A NOTE TO PARENTS

When your children are ready to "step into reading," giving them the right books—and lots of them—is as crucial as giving them the right food to eat. **Step into Reading Books** present exciting stories and information reinforced with lively, colorful illustrations that make learning to read fun, satisfying, and worthwhile. They are priced so that acquiring an entire library of them is affordable. And they are beginning readers with an important difference— they're written on four levels.

Step 1 Books, with their very large type and extremely simple vocabulary, have been created for the very youngest readers. **Step 2 Books** are both longer and slightly more difficult. **Step 3 Books,** written to mid-second-grade reading levels, are for the child who has acquired even greater reading skills. **Step 4 Books** offer exciting nonfiction for the increasingly proficient reader.

Children develop at different ages. **Step into Reading Books,** with their four levels of reading, are designed to help children become good—and interested—readers *faster*. The grade levels assigned to the four steps—preschool through grade 1 for Step 1, grades 1 through 3 for Step 2, grades 2 and 3 for Step 3, and grades 2 through 4 for Step 4—are intended only as guides. Some children move through all four steps very rapidly; others climb the steps over a period of several years. These books will help your child "step into reading" in style!

Photo credits: AP/Wide World Photos: p. 26; Brown Brothers: p. 4, 20, 32, 37, 43, 44; Library of Congress: p. 30; National Baseball Library and Archive: p. 8, 11, 15, 23, 28-29, 39, 40

Library of Congress Cataloging-in-Publication Data
Kramer, Sydelle.
Ty Cobb : bad boy of baseball / by S. A. Kramer.
  p. cm. — (Step into reading. A step 4 book)
ISBN: 0-679-87283-3 (pbk.) — ISBN: 0-679-97283-8 (lib. bdg.)
1. Cobb, Ty, 1886–1961—Juvenile literature. 2. Baseball players—United States—Biography—Juvenile literature. I. Title. II. Series: Step into reading. Step 4 book.
GV865.C6K73 1995
796.357'092—dc20
[B] 94-39675

Manufactured in the United States of America 10 9 8 7 6 5 4 3 2 1

STEP INTO READING is a trademark of Random House, Inc.

Step into Reading

TY COBB

Bad Boy of Baseball

By S. A. Kramer

A Step 4 Book

Random House New York

Mean Streak

Ball four! Ty Cobb walks. Suddenly the stadium crowd is excited. They know Ty will do anything to score. Only twenty-two years old, he's already baseball's smartest—and trickiest—player. Ty, the Detroit Tigers' center fielder, is the game's first superstar.

It's August 24, 1909. The Tigers are battling the Philadelphia Athletics. With Ty on first, the Athletics are nervous. They know he's fearless on the base paths, always daring fielders to throw him out. It's impossible to predict what he'll do next.

Suddenly he takes off! He steals second base easily. Then, an instant later, he charges toward third.

This time the Athletics are ready. The

catcher makes a perfect throw to third. But Ty isn't about to give up. He knows how to make it dangerous to tag him out.

Clenching his teeth, he slides hard into the bag. He kicks his right foot in the air, and aims his spikes at the third baseman. If the man tags him, Ty will hurt him. If he tries to dodge the spikes, Ty will be safe.

The third baseman doesn't back off. He tags Ty out. But Ty's spikes cut his arm.

The Athletics are angry. They know Ty doesn't care if he injures somebody. Later, their manager calls Ty "the dirtiest player in baseball."

It seems wherever Ty goes, trouble always follows. Still, if he's in the lineup, the game is sure to be exciting.

Who is this violent man fans flock to the ballpark to see? What makes baseball's biggest star so nasty?

Sports or School?

The Narrows, Georgia, December 18, 1886. A baby boy is born in a white farmhouse built on rich red soil. His father names him after an ancient city called Tyre. Under attack by an enemy, the people of Tyre fought to the last. Little Tyrus Raymond Cobb seems to have that same fighting spirit.

Ty is born into a world that's different from ours. His father marries his mother when she is only twelve. Ty grows up among people who lived through the Civil War, when states from the North fought states from the South. As a Southerner, he's taught that Northerners cannot be trusted. From childhood, he's raised to believe that

Ty Cobb in 1887, only a few months old.

whites are better than blacks.

Ty's father is an important man. He's the publisher of the newspaper and the head of all local schools. Ty, he dreams, will achieve even more. He'll be a doctor, a lawyer, or an army officer. The Professor, as Ty's dad is nicknamed, feels education is the key to success.

Ty adores his father. But he's not sure the Professor loves him. No matter what Ty does, his father never seems satisfied. Ty grows up feeling he constantly has to prove his worth.

Even as a child, he has a temper. In fifth grade, a classmate's goof costs Ty's team the spelling bee. Ty is so furious that he beats the boy up. Ty may be very young, but he already hates to lose.

Despite his father's hopes, Ty is not a top student. Still, there *is* something he's really good at—baseball. By the time he's fourteen, he's a local star. But the Professor isn't pleased—no game is as important as school.

When he was younger, all Ty wanted was his father's blessing. But now he needs to play baseball more than anything. He sews his own glove and carves his own bats. Then, when he's seventeen, he asks minor-league teams for a tryout. He does it in secret—he knows the Professor won't approve.

One club, the Augusta Tourists, invites him to try out. Ty tells his father, "I just have to go." The Professor is against it, yet allows Ty to leave home. But he warns Ty, "Don't come home a failure."

Ty makes the team. Still, he's not good enough yet for the majors. So he practices hard and studies the game. He feels if he becomes the best, his father will accept him. He also believes that to be great, he can't be a nice guy.

By the time he's eighteen, Ty's a top minor-league player. But he can't wait to

Ty (top row, third from right) *with the Augusta Tourists in 1905.*

reach the majors. So he writes letters praising himself to a famous sports reporter. He signs them with a fake name.

The trick works. The reporter writes stories about Ty. Soon the Detroit Tigers are interested in him. His dream is about to come true. Baseball will be his career. Now he'll make his father proud.

But then something terrible happens. On the night of August 9, 1905, Ty's mother is home alone. The Professor is out of town. Suddenly she hears someone trying to enter the house.

Mrs. Cobb is terrified. It's pitch-black in her bedroom. She can't see a thing, but she thinks a burglar is breaking in. Grabbing a shotgun, she fires twice.

Ty's mother has killed a man—but it turns out he's no thief. He's Ty's father, coming home early.

Less than three weeks later, the Tigers call Ty up. But getting to the majors doesn't fulfill his dream—the Professor won't ever see him play.

Ty is so upset about his father's death, he can't speak about it until he's much older. Then he says, "My father [was killed] when I was eighteen years old—*by a member of my own family.* I didn't get over that. I've never gotten over it."

Ty and his father didn't always get along. But Ty loved him very much. He always remembers the Professor's order: "Don't come home a failure." Ty vows not to.

The Rookie

August 30, 1905. The Tigers are playing the New York Highlanders. In the bottom of the first, Ty comes out on deck. This will be his first major-league at-bat.

Only eighteen years old, he's nervous but proud. He thinks his new uniform is the most beautiful thing he's ever seen. With his cap on, his thin red-blond hair is nearly invisible. He looks like a little boy, with his small ears sticking out from his head.

But as he waits on deck, Ty's face turns mean. He grits his teeth and sets his jaw. With his blue-gray eyes like slits, he stares out at the mound. He tells himself he hates the pitcher.

Ty hits left-handed. At the plate, he

*Ty shows off his batting stance shortly
after joining the Detroit Tigers.*

chokes up on his short, heavy bat. He keeps his hands more than three inches apart. His hitting style gives him good bat control—he can smack the ball anywhere he wants.

To be a great hitter, Ty knows he must be able to place the ball. He plays in the Dead Ball Era (1903–1919), when bat control counts for more than power. Hardly anyone slugs home runs—it's too hard to hit the ball far.

That's because the ball is heavier than today's. And pitchers can spit on it or scrape it. As the innings pass, the ball becomes wet, dirty, and hard to see. Yet only three to four new balls are used per game. Even fouls are thrown back from the stands.

With a heavy, dirty, wet ball, it's no wonder games are low-scoring. No team can count on a homer to win. Runs are produced with sacrifices, steals, bunts, and the hit-and-run. Victory belongs to the club with a scoring plan.

Ty is the perfect player for the Dead Ball Era. He's fast and has terrific bat control. He sizes up a situation and knows just what to do. Understanding the game is more important to him than power. A teammate says, "He didn't outhit and he didn't outrun them. He *outthought* them!"

Now Ty waits for the pitch. He forgets it's his first time up. There's a man on third he's determined to drive in. The pitcher delivers. Ty smashes the ball into left-center. He takes off from home so quickly that he makes it all the way to second. His first hit is a double. He also gets a run batted in.

But his quick start soon slows. He finishes the season with a batting average of just .240. Next year, he tells himself, he'll have to do better. He hasn't come this far only to fail.

Superstar

1906. It's Ty's second season. So far he's had a tough year. The Tigers don't treat him as an equal member of the team. In baseball, older players usually poke fun at brand-new ones. Ty's no longer a rookie, but his teammates still treat him like one.

All the Tigers are Northerners, so they tease Ty about his Southern accent. Whenever he speaks, they turn their backs on him. Some lock him out of the bathroom. Others won't let him take batting practice.

His mail is stolen. His clothes are tied in knots. One player cuts up his straw hat. Another saws his homemade bats in half.

The Tigers think their pranks are funny. But Ty feels they're picking on him. He believes his teammates are all against him. Unlike other players, he can't laugh off their tricks. Ty is cold and distant, with no sense of humor.

He starts to fight with his teammates. His temper is awful both on and off the field. He won't eat or room with anyone. At times he refuses to speak.

Ty's imagination runs wild. He believes he's in danger from his teammates. In order to protect himself, he gets a gun. Every night, he sleeps with it under his pillow.

To show the Tigers up, Ty's determined to prove his talent. If his father were alive, he'd expect nothing less. So Ty pushes himself to show just how good he is.

One morning he has his tonsils removed. Still, he takes the field that afternoon. His throat bleeds for three weeks afterward—but he's in the lineup every day.

It's important to Ty that everyone thinks

*Ty chats with the Philadelphia police chief late in the 1909
season. After spiking the Athletics' third baseman,
Ty needed police protection from angry fans.*

he's baseball's best. He himself admits, "I've
got to be first—in everything."

By the end of the season, Ty's average is

.320. He's such a good hitter, he's nicknamed the Georgia Peach. The next year he hits .350 and wins his first batting crown. His speed and his nerve make him a terror on the base paths. Even the Tigers who tease him realize he's become a star.

Ty is able to do things no one else can. Once he steals three bases on three pitches in a row. In game after game, he goes from first to third on a bunt. Often he scores from second on a groundout. One newspaper says, "With young Cobb in the game, there's never any telling what might happen."

Ty's not just skillful. He's also scary. He shouts insults at fielders, and slides at them with his spikes up. One says Ty came at him "like a lion out of a cage." Many are so afraid of him they make errors when he's on base. Some accuse him of sharpening his spikes before each game.

Pitchers especially fear him. Ty will do

anything to upset them. Once he bends over and waves his backside at a hurler. Another time, he refuses to face the mound. As the pitch comes in, he chats to the hitter on deck. Staring at Ty's back, the pitcher hurls four balls in a row.

Pitchers rarely throw at Ty. They know if they hit him, he'll take revenge. One afternoon, though, someone takes the risk. He throws hard at Ty's head, but misses. On the next pitch, Ty drags a bunt toward first. The hurler rushes to cover the bag. Ty plans to slide right into him.

But the pitcher realizes what Ty's going to do. He beats Ty to first—and keeps on running. He doesn't stop until he reaches the coaching box.

Ty comes after him. He runs out of the base path. With his spikes flashing, he leaps into the coaching box. The pitcher dives out of the way—and never throws at Ty again.

Ty in a studio portrait taken in 1906.

No other athlete has such a rough style. To Ty, "baseball is something like a war." He's accused of playing dirty, but he feels he's just playing to win. Some people insist he is insane.

Yet most fans feel Ty's given baseball a new kind of excitement. They may not like him as a person, but there's no one else they'd rather see. By 1908, he's the American League's biggest attraction. He may be a bully—but he's also a superstar.

Lonely at the Top

August 1908. The Tigers lead the pennant race by just one game. Suddenly, Ty disappears without a trace.

His teammates are angry. They don't like or trust him. It seems as if Ty has deserted the club.

They know he usually does what's best for himself, not the team. If he's in a slump, he refuses to play. If a pitcher gives him trouble, he may sit out the game. One day he won't take the field because he hates his hotel room.

But Ty has a secret he hasn't told the Tigers. He's in love with a seventeen-year-old woman named Charlie Lombard. Charlie's from Georgia too—Ty's gone home to

Ty and his family at home in 1923. Left to right: *Shirley, Ty, Ty Jr.* (standing), *Howell, Beverly, Charlie, and Herschel.*

get married. He's about to start a family.

Yet not even love and marriage make Ty a nicer guy. Just like his father, he has trouble showing affection. Baseball keeps him away from home much of the time. He doesn't understand how to be a family man.

Even after Ty and Charlie have children,

baseball is the first thing on Ty's mind. He puts everything he has into the sport. Nothing is as important.

His devotion is rewarded. By 1910, one owner calls Ty "the greatest player of all time." He's named the league's Most Valuable Player in 1911. A pitcher says Ty is "the most feared man in the history of baseball." He goes on to win the American League batting crown nine years in a row.

By the time he's twenty-four, Ty is the nation's most famous sports figure. There's no such thing as TV, yet almost every American knows his face. Newspapers all over the country headline his feats. In 1916, Ty becomes the first professional athlete to star in a film.

The longer he's in baseball, the richer he becomes. Ty knows how to bargain for salary increases. He soon becomes the sport's highest-paid player.

He uses his money wisely. In 1908, he
makes a deal with a small Georgia soda
company. No one's heard of Coca-Cola, but

Ty sends New York Highlanders' third baseman Jimmy Austin into the air as he slides in safely. This 1909 photo shows what opposing fielders were up against when Ty was on the base paths.

Ty likes its taste. When Coke becomes America's favorite soda, it makes Ty the first millionaire athlete.

Ty poses before a home game.

Money is extremely important to Ty. It's a way of showing off his success. But even though he's rich, he's very cheap. When he gets older, he uses candles instead of electric lights. He won't pay for a telephone, or buy firewood if it's cold. At times, Ty burns his fan mail for heat.

Baseball has brought Ty wealth and glory. Yet he's not a happy man. The game can't teach him how to get along with people. His success never makes him less angry.

All wrapped up in himself, Ty doesn't know how to be a friend. He can't even get close to his own family. As the seasons go by, he gets lonelier and lonelier.

Ty may be a hero to many fans, but he's hated by most players. On October 9, 1910, he finds out just how much.

It's the last day of the season. No one has won the American League batting crown yet. The race is between Ty and Cleveland's

Ty, with the look that put fear in the hearts of opposing pitchers.

Nap Lajoie. Today's doubleheaders will decide the winner.

Ty is sitting out the games. He's gone on

a trip with his wife. The Tigers are angry. They know Ty's keeping his average as high as possible by not playing. Once again, it seems as though he doesn't care whether the team wins.

Ty wants to win his fourth batting crown in a row. Yet he's so unpopular with the players, they're nearly all rooting for Nap. Today the St. Louis Browns are playing Nap's club. Some Browns decide to secretly help Nap win the title.

When Nap smacks a fly ball, the outfielder doesn't catch it. When he hits a slow grounder, the shortstop makes a weak throw to first. The third baseman stands so far back, Nap can easily lay down bunts. He gets six bunt singles in a row.

By the end of the day, Nap has eight hits. Now his average is higher than Ty's. Eight of Ty's own teammates send Nap a telegram congratulating him!

But the president of the American League realizes what's happened. He names Ty the true batting champ.*

Ty has taken home yet another title. But nothing can make him feel satisfied. He's at the top of the game, yet he's still afraid of failing. And now he's convinced he's all alone.

* Many years pass before the league finds it made a mistake. It counted Ty's hits incorrectly—Nap really should have won the title.

Older, but Not Wiser

Spring training, 1917. Ty is thirty years old, and as mean as ever. Today's game is just for practice—still, he spikes a fielder on purpose. The man is so angry he comes to Ty's hotel room to slug it out.

A crowd watches closely. The two take their shirts off. The man punches Ty and knocks him to his knees. But when Ty gets up, he never goes down again. He gives the man two black eyes and a bloody nose.

Even though Ty is older, he's still picking fights. He frequently gets thrown out of games. He screams at umpires, shoves them, and throws dirt at them. One time he runs to an ump's dressing room and tries to beat him up.

Ty goes after fans, too. In 1912, a man sitting behind third base insults him. One of the fan's hands is missing. The other hand has only two fingers.

Ty jumps into the seats and knocks the man down. Another fan shouts that the man has no hands. Ty yells out, "I don't care if he has no feet." Then Ty stamps on the man's face with his spikes.

Ty often picks on black people. Many whites of his time are prejudiced—blacks are not even allowed to play in the major leagues. But Ty is much worse than most.

One day he walks down a street that a black worker is paving. When the man complains about where Ty is stepping, Ty turns around and socks him.

Another time, he slaps a black stadium worker when the man tries to shake his hand. He slugs a black elevator operator and stabs a black night watchman. In a hotel one

Ty crosses the plate ahead of a teammate.

night, he kicks a black maid in the stomach.

No matter what Ty does, though, the fans keep coming to watch him play. For many of them, Ty *is* baseball. They admire his tricks, his speed—even his violence. But then, in 1920, a man named Babe Ruth changes everything.

Unlike Ty, the Babe slugs homer after homer. While Ty figures out a scoring plan, the Babe just swings with all his might. The Babe's power makes Ty's style of placing the ball seem old-fashioned. Once fans thrilled to Ty's perfect bunts. Now they just want to see the ball clear the fence.

The Babe quickly becomes baseball's greatest star. Ty feels forgotten—teams no longer want smart players like him. But though the game has changed, he doesn't quit. Baseball is his life. In 1921, he starts managing the Tigers. He also keeps playing for them.

By 1925, Ty is thirty-eight years old. The Babe and his homers have taken over the game. One afternoon Ty can't bear to hear about the Babe again. So he announces: "Today…for the first time in my career, I

*Ty's famous hands-apart grip, as seen during
an at-bat in Washington, D.C., in 1922.*

will be deliberately going for home runs."
Ty's going to show he too can be a slugger.

In the next two games, he gets nine hits

Ty placing the ball right where he wants it.

in a row. He wallops five homers, one double, and three singles. A superb hitter, he can still do anything with the bat. But once he's proved he can hit for power, he won't do it again. To him, baseball will always be a thinking-man's game.

Ty finally retires when he's forty-two. He leaves with the highest lifetime batting average ever—.367. There's no doubt he is one of baseball's greatest hitters. He's especially proud to be one of the first five men elected to the Hall of Fame.

After Baseball

Without baseball, Ty feels lost. He has always given himself to it completely. Nothing makes him feel better—not even his family. He's not close to any of his five children. He and his oldest son barely talk to each other.

As Ty gets older, his family life falls apart. He and his wife, Charlie, divorce in 1947. Two years later, he marries a woman named Frances. But suddenly, two of his sons die young. Then, in 1956, Frances leaves him. No one can live happily with Ty.

Baseball is no longer a part of Ty's life. Now he feels he can't count on his family. He has only one thing left—a lot of money. He doesn't spend it on himself. Yet as he

Ty poses with his second wife, Frances, in 1949.
They would get divorced seven years later.

gets older, he does become more generous to others.

He gives money to needy retired ball-

Ty and fellow old-timer Tris Speaker
meet Yankee star Joe DiMaggio.

players. In his hometown in Georgia, he builds a new hospital. He starts a fund for poor college students and names it after his father.

Yet Ty is more unhappy than ever. A lonely man, he begins to drink heavily. Very few athletes ever come to visit him. All he has are his memories.

He even says he'd give up all his money if only he could change how players feel about him. He knows no one has forgotten how nasty he could be.

Ty dies of cancer at the age of seventy-four. Only three baseball players come to his funeral. He may have been the game's most exciting athlete ever—but he was not a good man.

Still, for over twenty years, Ty was one of baseball's best. He set forty-three records in his long career. He left his mark on the game as few others have. As one player said, "To see him was to remember him forever."

TYRUS RAYMOND (TY) COBB
The Georgia Peach

Born December 18, 1886—Died July 17, 1961

Career: 1905–1920 for the Detroit Tigers

1921–26 player-manager for Detroit

1927–28 for the Philadelphia Athletics

Position: Center field, right field

6'1", 175 pounds

Batted left-handed. Threw right-handed.

Hall of Fame

• Feats •

1. First in lifetime batting average (.367) and runs scored (2,245).
2. Second in total hits (4,191) and triples (297).
3. Third in stolen bases—892.
4. Fourth in total bases (5,854), doubles (724), total games played (3,034), and total at-bats (11,429).
5. Fifth in total RBIs—1,961.
6. Eighth in total extra-base hits—1,136.
7. Won twelve American League batting crowns, including nine in a row and twelve in thirteen years. He won his first title when he was just twenty.
8. Batted over .400 three times.
9. Batted over .300 twenty-three times.

10. Had 200 or more hits in a season nine times.
11. Stole second, third, and home in the same inning four times.
12. Won the American League Triple Crown, 1909.
13. Won the American League Most Valuable Player Award, 1911.
14. Second in outfield assists (throwing a runner out from the outfield)—392, but most outfield errors ever—271.
15. Got the most votes of the first five men elected to the Hall of Fame—more, even, than Babe Ruth.

• Greatest Feat •

In 1911, Ty batted .420, with 144 RBIs, 147 runs scored, 248 hits, and 83 stolen bases. He led the league in doubles, triples, and slugging percentage. Many say this is one of the greatest seasons ever.